MORGAN HORSE

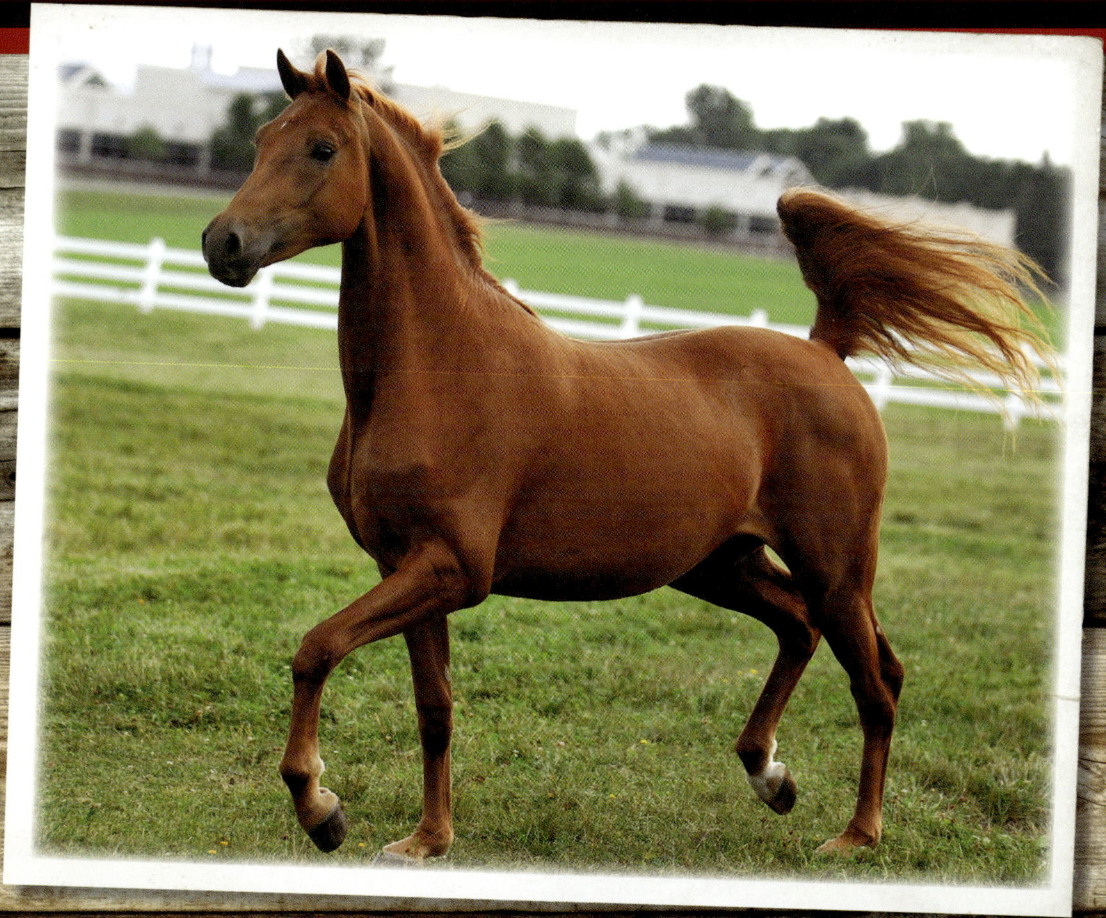

EZ READERS

Marylou Morano Kjelle

Creating Young Nonfiction Readers

EZ Readers lets children delve into nonfiction at beginning reading levels. Young readers are introduced to new concepts, facts, ideas, and vocabulary.

Tips for Reading Nonfiction with Beginning Readers

Talk about Nonfiction
Begin by explaining that nonfiction books give us information that is true. The book will be organized around a specific topic or idea, and we may learn new facts through reading.

Look at the Parts
Most nonfiction books have helpful features. Our *EZ Readers* include a Contents page, an Index, and color photographs. Share the purpose of these features with your reader.

Contents
Located at the front of a book, the Contents displays a list of the big ideas within the book and where to find them.

Index
An Index is an alphabetical list of topics and the page numbers where they are found.

Photos/Charts
A lot of information can be found by "reading" the charts and photos found within nonfiction text. Help your reader learn more about the different ways information can be displayed.

With a little help and guidance about reading nonfiction, you can feel good about introducing a young reader to the world of *EZ Readers* nonfiction books.

Mitchell Lane
PUBLISHERS

2001 SW 31st Avenue
Hallandale, FL 33009
www.mitchelllane.com

First Edition, 2021.

Author: Marylou Morano Kjelle
Designer: Ed Morgan
Editor: Morgan Brody

Names/credits:
Title: Morgan Horse / by Marylou Morano Kjelle
Description: Hallandale, FL :
Mitchell Lane Publishers, [2021]

Series: Popular Horse Breeds
Library bound ISBN: 978-1-68020-569-5
eBook ISBN: 978-1-68020-570-1

EZ readers is an imprint of Mitchell Lane Publishers.

Photo credits: Freepik.com, Shutterstock

CONTENTS

Words in **bold** can be found in the Glossary.

Morgan Horses are strong. They are fast and powerful.

Morgans are short horses. Their shoulders are strong. Their heads are short and broad. Their necks are long.

Their eyes are wide and large. They have pointed ears.

Did You Know?

All Morgan Horses share an **ancestor** born in Massachusetts in the 1700's.

Most Morgan Horses have dark **coats** although they come in many colors. They have no white marks above the **hock**. There can be white marks on their face.

Their tail is long and flowing. Sometimes it touches the ground. Morgan Horses eat grass, hay, corn, and oats.

Did You Know?

Both sides of the Civil War used Morgan Horses as **cavalry** mounts.

Morgans weigh from 800 to 1,200 pounds (362–544 kg). They are about 60 inches (168 cm) tall.

DID YOU KNOW?

Morgan Horses were also used by the **Pony Express** in the 1860's. They pulled **stagecoaches** in pioneer times.

It takes about 330 days (11 months) for a Morgan **foal** to be born. Morgan Horses live about 30 years.

DID YOU KNOW?

Some Morgan Horses have lived as long as 45 years.

They are good hunters and jumpers.
People ride them for fun.

The Morgan is a gentle horse that is easy to care for. Morgan Horses live in the United States and throughout the world.

Did You Know?

The Morgan Horse is the state animal for Vermont and the state horse of Massachusetts.

GLOSSARY

ancestor
A person or animal's family background

cavalry
Soldiers who fight on horses

coat
The outer covering of fur, hair, or wool on an animal

foal
A baby horse

hock
A joint in the lower leg of a horse

Pony Express
An early way of delivering mail using a rider on a horse

stagecoach
A carriage drawn by horses that carried mail and people

Sources

"American Morgan Horse." *International Museum of the Horse*. http://imh.org/exhibits/online/breeds-of-the-world/north-america/american-morgan-horse/

Draper, Judith. *The Complete Horse Book: The Ultimate Guide to Horse Breeds and a Practical Horse Care Manual*. London: Anness Publishing Limited, 1996

Dutson, Judith. *Storey's Illustrated Guide to 96 Horse Breeds of North America*. North Adams, MA: Storey Publishers, 2005.

Edwards, Elwyn Hartley. *Ultimate Horse*. New York: Dorling Kindersley, 2002.

Harris, Moira C. *America's Horses: A Celebration of the Horse Breeds Born in the USA*. Guilford, CT: Lyons Press, 2003.

"Mare Gestation Calculator." *The Horse*. Thehorse.com.

"What Makes a Morgan Horse So Special?" *Horsy Land*. www.horsyland.com/what-makes-a-morgan-horse-so-special

Further Reading

Web Pages

American Morgan Horse Association
https://www.morganhorse.com

Layos, Allie. "Everything You Need to Know About the Morgan Horse." *Wide Open Pets*. https://www.wideopenpets.com/all-you-need-to-know-about-the-morgan-horse/

"The Morgan Horse." *Crestmoon Morgans*. https://crescentmoonmorgans.com/the-morgan-horse

Books

DK. *The Everything Book of Horses and Ponies* (Everything About Pets) London, DK, 2019.

Field, Ellen F. *Justin Morgan and the Big Horse Race*. Goshen, MA: Willow Bend Publishing, 2013.

Meister, Carl. *Morgan Horses*, Mankato, MN: Amicus Books, 2018.

INDEX

ABOUT THE AUTHOR

Marylou Morano Kjelle lives and writes in Central New Jersey. She is a retired college English professor and the author of over 50 books on various topics for children and young adults. She learned a lot about the Morgan Horse while researching and writing this book. Marylou especially enjoyed learning about the role of Morgans in the Civil War.